CYRIL BONHAMY
AND THE
GREAT DRAIN
ROBBERY

A Red Fox Book

Published by Random House Children's Books
20 Vauxhall Bridge Road, London SW1V 2SA

A division of Random House UK Ltd
London Melbourne Sydney Auckland
Johannesburg and agencies throughout the world

1 3 5 7 9 10 8 6 4 2

First published in Great Britain by
Jonathan Cape Ltd 1983

Red Fox edition 1991
This Red Fox edition 1999

Printed and bound in Norway by
AIT Trondheim AS

RANDOM HOUSE UK Limited Reg. No. 954009

ISBN 0 09 975140 2

CYRIL BONHAMY
AND THE
GREAT DRAIN
ROBBERY

Jonathan Gathorne-Hardy

Illustrated by Quentin Blake

RED FOX

For Dee

Contents

Cyril and the Beebles

'Oh, Cyril — I can see this is going to be the most wonderful holiday we've ever had,' said Deirdre, squeezing some more sun-tan cream out of the tube.

'Why?' said Cyril irritably.

They had only been at Nice in the South of France three days and already his nose was bright red from sunburn. Deirdre had made a little tent of white paper for it which she'd stuck on with Elastoplast. It made Cyril feel ridiculous.

'Look, darling,' said Deirdre, 'you've been under that umbrella all morning. You must be boiling. Why don't you go and have a little swim? You'll feel better.' She reached out a loving hand to rub some more cream on to the plump white tummy of her husband lying beside her.

'Don't,' said Cyril, squirming away. He already

felt like some sort of meal because of all the suntan cream on him. But it was true he did feel very hot. He stood up, shoved his feet into his rope-soled shoes and stumped wearily towards the distant sea.

Cyril parked his shoes neatly on the beach where the waves broke. Then he nervously put one pink toe into the grey water. Although it was so hot that it was almost impossible to walk on the sand without shoes, the sea was surprisingly cold. It took him ten minutes, wincing and gasping, before he finally managed to get in completely.

For a while it was quite pleasant. Cyril could only swim on his back, and what he really enjoyed was floating.

But after a while he noticed a piece of tomato skin in the sea beside him. Then another. Then he saw half a carrot and a whole lot of little pieces like mince. All at once he realized the sea around him was completely filled with old food. He might as well have been floating in a stew.

Cyril began to swim agitatedly for the shore. It wasn't just food — there were huge lumps of this and that, bits of uncurling paper, burst balloons, specks and flecks and fragments, blobs.

'Ough — how *revolting*,' thought Cyril, staggering over the pebbles and on to the sand again, 'I hope I didn't swallow any of it.'

He seemed to have landed farther down the shore, because there was no sign of his shoes.

Cyril walked a hundred yards up the beach, and

then two hundred yards back. His shoes had vanished.

He chose a spot as nearly opposite Deirdre and their umbrella as he could and said politely to a large, fat man lying on his back, 'Excuse me, but have you seen my shoes?'

The fat man sat up and turned out to be a fat woman with very short black hair and sunglasses. She looked at Cyril and after a moment said, *'Je ne parle pas anglais.'*

Cyril smiled at her. 'Mon shoes,' he said. 'Not ici. Avey vous seen mon shoes?'

'Comment?' said the woman.

'Le clogs,' said Cyril, waving one of his feet at her. 'Le boots. *Où est?* Where are they — le feet?'

The fat woman took off her sunglasses and stared at him. *'Comment?'* she said again.

Cyril drew a deep breath, and did a little dance, pointing at his feet. 'Le clogs, le clogs, le clogs,' he cried. And then, suddenly exhausted, he said, 'Oh, forget it.' He'd begun to feel his usual feeling of baffled annoyance that the French, after all these centuries, still didn't really understand their own language.

The run back to Deirdre across the blazing hot sand was agony and caused some disturbance. Cyril had to jump for relief on to people's towels and clothes. Sometimes, by mistake, he jumped on to the people themselves. In his haste a good deal of sand got kicked over them. They yelled at him in French and some shook their fists at him.

10

'Was that nice, darling?' asked Deirdre, as he collapsed panting under the umbrella.

'No, it was not nice,' gasped Cyril, trying to get back his breath. 'It was frightful. Do you realize all the sewage of Nice empties into the sea here? It's disgusting.'

'You *must* try and keep your nose covered,' said Deirdre, reaching into her bag. 'It won't get better otherwise.'

'I don't know about my nose,' said Cyril, unwillingly letting her stick another tent of paper on his face. 'But my feet are agony. I'm not sure I can walk. Someone stole my shoes.'

'Never mind, dear,' said Deirdre. 'We'll buy some more later.'

After a while Cyril said, for the hundreth time, 'Don't you think it extraordinary how badly the French speak their own language?'

'Yes, dear,' said Deirdre soothingly.

After a large lunch and a snooze in their comfortable room at the Hotel Splendide, Cyril said his feet and his nose — indeed his whole body — were too sore for him to go on the beach again. He'd spend the afternoon in La Bibliothèque de Nice. La Bibliothèque de Nice was the Nice Public Library, just across the road from the Hotel Splendide. It was a huge, grand, cool building containing two million books.

Cyril only really liked books. He wrote books, he read books, he talked about books on telly, he bought books; very occasionally, when forced by Deirdre, he sold books. He would have liked nothing better than to wander all day in the vast, cool rooms of La Bibliothèque de Nice among millions of books — if it hadn't been for the difficulty over the illuminated Bibles.

La Bibliothèque de Nice was famous for its very old Bibles, painted by monks hundreds of years ago in the fourteenth century. Two days before, Cyril had tried to see them. For some extraordinary reason, he hadn't been allowed to.

Very soon a row had developed. It was made worse because the staff of La Bibliothèque de Nice had turned out to be even more hopeless at French than most people in France. Cyril had started to shout and wave his arms. Finally he had shouted, 'Is there no one in this library who speaks French?' And, after waiting a moment and getting no reply from the astonished staff, he had stormed out.

Much the same had happened yesterday. Cyril had become so angry it was only with great difficulty he had prevented himself from strangling the assistant.

This afternoon he determined to be more careful. He would chat to them. Be cool. At the same time, he would be firm.

He was pleased to see a different assistant at the desk. Cyril walked up. Quite a hot day, he said. The assistant agreed politely. Cyril, speaking fluent French, described his morning on the beach. Then, at the very end, very casually, he asked if he might see the Bibles.

'*Pardon, m'sieur, mais non,*' said the assistant.

'*Non?*' said Cyril. 'Why *non?*'

'Because, it so 'appen . . .' began the assistant.

'Please speak French,' said Cyril. '*Parlez français.*'

'Per'aps, if *monsieur* would allow,' said the assistant, 'it would be easier in Eeenglish. I speek Eeenglish.'

'I know you speak English,' said Cyril. 'You speak English very badly indeed. Luckily, I speak fluent French. Now listen carefully. I wish — I *weesh* — to see — *voir* le *Beebles*. The medieval Beebles. Why is it no possible de *voir* le Beebles?'

'Because, *monsieur*,' said the assistant, beginning to feel rather weary, 'les *Beebles*, as you call them . . .'

'Speak French, speak French,' snapped Cyril.

And so the assistant very carefully and slowly explained to Cyril, in French, that some Beebles had been stolen. They were fitting a new alarm system. Until then the Beeble room was closed.

Cyril didn't at first understand a word he was saying. But gradually he understood that the assistant was accusing him of planning to steal the Beebles. He was calling him a thief. Very angry, but just managing to control himself, Cyril leant over the counter. 'I think you should know,' he said, 'that I know a lot of very important people in the book world. I shall tell them about your outrageous accusation. How dare you. I very much doubt, young man, that you will be here very much longer.'

But back at the Hotel Splendide he calmed down. There had so far been only one difficulty at the hotel. When they arrived, Cyril and Deirdre discovered they had been put down as Monsieur and Madame Pomme de Terre. Once the mistake had been explained (Cyril had booked the rooms by telephone from England), everything had been perfect. Their room was large and overlooked the sea. There was a telly in one of the lounges. There was even a little hotel library.

But above all, the food was delicious. Supper that night had been superb — poached croquettes of frog, lobster, two bottles of white wine. Deirdre said she was sure the man at La Bibliothèque de Nice hadn't meant that Cyril was planning to steal the Bibles. It was a mistake — like Mr and Mrs Pomme de Terre. Cyril agreed.

After supper Deirdre went up to bed. Cyril said he'd just read the papers first. He hardly noticed the tall, dark Frenchman sitting behind a pot of palms as he strolled, a large glass of brandy in his hand, towards the telly room.

Had he known, he might have looked more closely. He might even have decided to leave the hotel altogether. For this was none other than Pierre Melon, the most dangerous criminal in France.

Pierre Melon — had a French gendarme come into the room at that moment, he would have shot him on sight. Not three weeks before, Pierre Melon, surrounded by gendarmes, had leapt from a court

14

window on to a motorbike twenty feet below and roared to freedom. A year before he had stolen the famous statue of the Venus de Milo — still not recovered: just one of hundreds of daring crimes that had put a price of half a million francs on his head. And as Cyril waddled past, Pierre Melon's black eyes glittered.

Whenever he went to a hotel, Pierre would do a bit of bribing. Sometimes he'd bribe all the waiters; sometimes just a dozen or so. Although the mistake about Cyril and Deirdre had been explained, they were still down in the books of the Hotel Splendide as Monsieur and Madame Pomme de Terre. That very evening one of the youngest and newest of the waiters bribed by Pierre — a mere boy — had told him Mr Pomme de Terre was really called Cyril Bonhamy. The news had amazed Pierre and excited him. Because he was interested in Cyril Bonhamy — very interested indeed.

A year or so before, Cyril had had a rather curious time being Father Christmas in a big store. Almost by accident, he had been responsible for the capture and arrest of the dangerous international criminal Madam Big.

This had got back to France, though not entirely correctly. Pierre remembered it — two rival criminal gangs, one led by Bonhamy, one by Madam Big. There had been a terrible battle. The Bonhamy gang had won.

Pierre looked through the leaves of the palm tree. So this was the great Cyril Bonhamy — astonishing.

Pierre could not disguise the evil-looking scar down one cheek; but he did at least wear a thick black wig. This Bonhamy — his only disguise was a little tent of paper on his nose. Amazing. Such courage would be useful when you were about to carry out the most dangerous and daring raid of your life. Especially when your right-hand man had just collapsed with crab poisoning.

Pierre looked carefully round the lounge, then pulled the wig low down over his forehead until it almost touched his eyebrows.

Arriving at Cyril's sofa, he bowed low and said, 'Excuse me — but can I 'ave the honour of meeting so distinguished an Eeengleeshman?'

Cyril looked up from the telly. 'Of course. How do you do?'

Pierre sat down and leant very close to Cyril. 'So,' he said. 'It ees like thees — no? Madam Beeg — she was in your way. You do not like. So — pouf! You cleeck the fingers. And Madam Beeg 'as gone. No?'

'No,' said Cyril. But then, pleased and surprised that his little adventure was so well known, he agreed that, well, yes, in a way it was more or less like that, sort of.

At this, glancing swiftly round the lounge, Pierre fixed his eyes meaningfully on Cyril's nose; then, to Cyril's intense surprise, he suddenly whipped off all his hair and whispered dramatically — 'Pierre Melon!'

'Goodness!' said Cyril, staring at Mr Melon's

16

completely bald head. But then, feeling ridiculous in the little tent of paper, at which Pierre was still staring, he pulled it off and said, 'Cyril Bonhamy.'

At once Pierre waved his hands grandly for champagne, replaced his wig, and cried, 'Ah — the great Mr Bonhamy.'

'Oh, you're too kind,' said Cyril modestly. 'A few books, an article or two . . .'

Pierre filled their glasses. '*À votre santé,*' he said.

'A *votre* santey, Mr Melon,' said Cyril.

'So — you speak French,' said Pierre, still more delighted. '*Vous parlez français?*'

'Oh, wee,' said Cyril airily. 'Wee, wee.'

Pierre now put his mouth close to Cyril's ear and began to talk very rapidly in French. Cyril nodded and said 'wee' without the faintest idea what he was talking about, until suddenly he heard the words Bibliothèque de Nice. At once everything became clear.

This charming man was obviously a high official, probably even the Director of the Nice Public Library. He had heard of Cyril's difficulty over le Beebles. He had come to apologise and arrange a special visit. At one point, Pierre unrolled a map of little roads and streets. Some of them seemed to be rivers. This baffled Cyril, until he realized it was a map of *medieval* Nice, the time when le Beebles were painted.

'Wee,' said Cyril, nodding and smiling, 'wee, wee, wee.'

'And so,' finished Pierre, 'we meet here tomorrow night at the same time? That is agreed?'

'Wee,' said Cyril, 'I'm delighted.'

Pierre reached out his hand and gently replaced the piece of paper on Cyril's sun-burnt nose. 'Permit me,' he said politely.

And thinking to himself, what dash, what bravery, to sit there without his disguise, he bowed low and hurried swiftly from the lounge.

As Cyril undressed he said casually to Deirdre, 'Sorry to be late, darling. Been having a talk with the Director of the Bibliothèque de Nice. He's arranged for me to see the Beebles tomorrow.'

'Mmmm,' said Deirdre sleepily.

'Charming fellow,' said Cyril, doing up his pink pyjamas. 'Read all my books. Spoke almost perfect French,' and he got into bed, thinking it had really been quite a good day after all.

He might have been less contented had he known he was about to begin one of the most terrifying adventures of his whole life.

The Terrible Truth!

Promptly at eleven o'clock the next night Pierre appeared in the telly lounge of the Hotel Splendide.

'Isn't it rather late to see Bibles?' Deirdre had asked.

'Oh no, not in France,' Cyril had said. 'Besides, he probably doesn't want to embarrass his staff.'

Bold as he was, Pierre had not quite dared to set out on the most daring robbery of his career disguised only in a wig. He had added a large ginger moustache and dark glasses.

He was deeply impressed, therefore, to see that the great Cyril Bonhamy — the most wanted criminal in England — still had no more than the little tent of white paper covering his nose.

As Cyril came up, Pierre couldn't help pointing at his nose. 'Such courage!' he said admiringly.

'Courage?' said Cyril, slightly nettled. 'I don't

see it takes much courage. But my wife Deirdre feels . . .' He didn't finish because Pierre had turned away and was clicking his fingers at one of the waiters. 'Anyway,' thought Cyril, 'I don't really think your appearance is suitable for the Director of the Bibliothèque de Nice.' However, he was too polite to say anything about the ginger moustache. Too polite, as well, to ask Pierre why on earth he was wearing gum boots.

The waiter returned carrying a small wicker suitcase. At once Pierre set off towards the foyer of the hotel. 'Come,' he said over his shoulder, 'we 'ave very leetle time.'

Outside the Hotel Splendide there was another surprise. Standing in the warm night air under a street lamp, the Director of the Bibliothèque de Nice put his fingers in his mouth and gave a low whistle. Instantly, two large figures came silently from the shadows and joined them.

Cyril supposed they were visiting professors, except they simply looked like two thugs. They were dressed in sweaters and jeans and were also wearing gum boots. They were each carrying sacks bulging with — what? Perhaps they had brought more Beebles to add to the collection.

One was called Gaston Something, the other Michel Something-else. Gaston Something was short and thick, with short hair and very few teeth. Cyril smiled at him and pointed at his sack.

'Beebles?' he said politely.

'Huh?' said Gaston.

'You avez le Beebles?' repeated Cyril. 'La belle medieval Beebles?'

Gaston just grunted, turned away and spat into the gutter. He and Michel hadn't liked the idea of bringing someone else in on this job. Not even a top English robber. Now he saw the top English robber he liked it still less. To Cyril's disgust, he spat again.

Pierre crossed the wide, almost empty street towards the Bibliothèque de Nice. But on the other side, instead of continuing up the broad steps and in through the large doors of the library, Pierre stopped on the pavement.

He seemed to be waiting for an old man on a bicycle to pass out of sight. When he had done so, and the long street was completely empty, Pierre was handed a metal rod by Gaston. To Cyril's astonishment, he then began to lever up a manhole cover in the pavement.

When it was open, Gaston and Michel disappeared inside it. Pierre handed Cyril a torch and whispered, 'Queeck.' With some difficulty Cyril got through the hole and down a steep iron ladder. He could hear Pierre following him, and a clang as the manhole cover fell into place. They were in darkness.

At the bottom of the ladder, the three other men stood talking excitedly in French, looking at some sort of plan. Cyril flashed his torch about.

From the space around the bottom of the ladder he could see the round openings of four tunnels.

Clearly, these were old medieval tunnels, one of which was an underground way of getting into the library and the room with the Beebles. There was a sound of dripping. The air was warm and smelt rather unpleasant.

After a while the three Frenchmen decided which was the right tunnel. Pierre turned his torch on Cyril.

'Come, my friend — now we are on our way,' he said. He spoke English as it had already become clear to him that he would not get far speaking French to Cyril. 'I will lead. Gaston and Michel next. My friend — Cyril Bonhamy — will bring up the rear. *Allons-y!* Let us go!' And shining his torch to the front, he led them boldly down the middle tunnel.

Quite soon it seemed to Cyril that, although it might be an old underground tunnel leading to the Beebles, it also ran, for part of the way at least, beside one of Nice's sewers.

He trotted to catch the tall figure of Professor Michel striding ahead of him and eventually managed to tap him on the back. '*Excusez-moi,* Professor,' he said, 'but est a sewer ici here? Sewer — wee?'

Professor Michel didn't even bother to stop, but just turned his thin, hawk-like face and said, 'Huh?'

Cyril flashed his torch on the black stream running slowly beside them. 'Est la sewarge?' he said. 'Drainage — baths — wee? Sewarge? La sewarge, je theenk.'

But Professor Michel was as rude as Professor Gaston. He too simply grunted and spat.

In fact, Cyril realized that the question wasn't necessary. There was simply no doubt at all about it being a sewer. The smell was growing steadily worse. And if you looked closely you could actually see chunks of la sewarge bobbing about in the black stream.

After half an hour, when they were beside yet another sewer, he realized it was not just sewers part of the way. It was all sewers and only sewers. It suddenly dawned on Cyril that sewers were the whole point.

There had been a most embarrassing mistake. Pierre Melon and these men were nothing to do with Beebles at all but belonged to some sort of club for exploring sewers. It was clearly something the French loved. That was why the sea was full of la sewarge. It was like those people you read about in England who went down underground tunnels and holes in Yorkshire to get trapped. Gloomily, Cyril trudged along behind Michel and wondered how long looking at sewers went on.

After an hour it became plain the club was lost. In front of them three tunnels branched off the one they were in. Pierre and the others looked at the plan and talked excitedly among themselves. Finally, Pierre came up to Cyril.

'Mr Bonhamy, please 'elp us. Wheech of these routes do you think we should take?'

Cyril looked wearily at the plan. If you liked

sewers, which he didn't, he couldn't see it made the slightest difference which one you looked at. 'That one,' he said, pointing to the right-hand tunnel.

'You see!' said Pierre triumphantly to the others. 'Per'aps, Mr Bonhamy, you would be so kind as to lead us.'

'All right — if you insist,' said Cyril, too tired to speak French.

He plodded ahead of them down the tunnel, followed by Gaston, Michel and finally Pierre. 'I'll have to make some sort of excuse and get out of this,' he thought. He saw now why the others were in gum boots. His comfortable rope-soled shoes had gone soggy and begun to fall apart.

The tunnel grew narrower and lower. Cyril bent down, too late to prevent his head dislodging a lump of la sewarge. Cyril bent lower, but still the tunnel grew smaller. Cyril bent double, then dropped on to his hands and knees and crawled. Before long he was forcing himself down something little better than a pipe.

It grew almost too small to continue. He was about to turn back when he saw by the light of his torch that, beyond a still narrower bit ahead, the sewer seemed to widen out.

He lay flat and shouted loudly, 'Push me. Pushez-moi, *s'il vous plaît*.'

Gaston must have been extremely strong. Cyril felt big hands on his sodden feet and then he suddenly shot forward until the sewer tunnel gripped him on all sides and he could go no farther.

He could also not go back. He pushed with his hands; then he pulled with his hands. He was stuck.

'Help!' shouted Cyril, beating his hands against the slimy walls of the pipe. 'Oh suckors — help — suckors — help! help! help!' He kicked his feet and beat his hands more and more wildly. Once, he felt his foot stroke something soft behind him and he thought he heard a sharp but muffled cry. 'Oh suckors,' shouted Cyril.

Finally, exhausted, he lay still. After a few minutes he felt someone tie a rope round his ankles and moments later, with much painful scraping, they yanked him back.

Standing in the first sewer, Cyril looked at himself in dismay.

'*Courage, mon brave,*' said Pierre, putting out his hand to clap him on the back and then withdrawing it. 'It is worth it — no? Well worth it.'

'I can't say it is,' said Cyril, crossly. 'It's all very well for you — but look at me!' He looked at himself. He was more or less covered in la sewarge from head to foot.

But Pierre had already turned away and was discussing their route with the others. (It gave Cyril some slight satisfaction to see that Gaston's nose was bleeding.)

This time they took the middle sewer and after about half an hour had apparently reached their destination.

To Cyril, it just looked like any other part of any

other awful French sewer. But now Gaston and Michel became extremely busy. They took several lumps of what Cyril recognized as explosives out one of the sacks and began to fix them to the sewer ceiling. Into these they stuck the end of a long wire which was wound round a roller.

At last, thought Cyril, they're doing something sensible. No doubt if you get lost in the sewers you are allowed to sort of explode yourself free. Embarrassing, he thought, if you exploded yourself into someone's bathroom.

Gaston unwound the wire and they all went and crouched down where the sewer turned a corner. Gaston fixed the end of the wire into a small box. Then he pushed a plunger on the top.

There was a short pause, then the echoing *Crrrrump* of an explosion.

Bricks were everywhere, and a good deal of la sewarge had been blown about. But a fair-sized jagged hole had been blown in the roof. They all looked up — Cyril could see no sign of the street in the blackness above.

He became aware that the three men were looking at him. Pierre coughed. 'Excuse me, Mr Bonhamy,' he said, 'but you are not as 'eavy as the rest of us. If we could leeft you up, you tie this rope somewhere — yes?'

'I suppose so,' said Cyril, taking the coil of rope. 'Be careful.'

Careful, however, is just what Gaston and Michel were not. They bent down, gripped Cyril on each side by leg and arm, counted — *un, deux, trois* — and simply threw him up into the air.

Cyril may not have been as heavy as the others, but he was certainly not light. He shot straight up through the hole, and came straight down again. Fortunately he landed with some force on top of Gaston, who collapsed with a loud cry.

'It's all right,' said Cyril, struggling off Gaston's head. 'I don't seem to be hurt.'

Gaston, however, was both hurt and furious. He jumped to his feet, pressing his handkerchief to his nose, which was bleeding again. 'II★??XZ?' he shouted in French. 'O!! XZZ? ★★'OI!?' He shook his fist and stepped forward. Luckily, Pierre and Michel held him back.

'It's your own stupid fault,' said Cyril crossly. 'You shouldn't have thrown me up like that. What did you expect me to do — fly? Je ne suis an bird, you know.'

This time they lifted him carefully up through the hole and Cyril managed to pull himself on to the floor of the room they'd exploded into.

By the light of his torch he saw a number of boxes, obviously scattered by the explosion. The door had a rather odd handle — a short steel bar. Cyril tied one end of the rope to it and dropped the other through the hole. Moments later the three other men had pulled themselves up and Pierre had found the light switch.

It was not a very large room. The walls were lined with shelves covered with metal boxes. Some of the metal boxes on the floor had been burst open by the explosion, scattering their contents. Necklaces, rings, bracelets, some with huge diamonds and rubies, lay everywhere.

Then, and during the next five minutes, Cyril realized the terrible truth. These men were not learned professors interested in Beebles. Nor were they members of a club for exploring sewers. They were robbers — and robbers, he could now see, of the most dangerous and violent sort.

He couldn't understand why he hadn't noticed before. Gaston looked particularly brutal. His eyes were very close together, like a pig's. It seemed to be hot work, ripping open the metal boxes. He'd taken off his coat and Cyril saw he carried a gun in a shoulder holster.

' 'Ere — you must 'ave the gloves,' said Pierre, throwing a pair of thin leather gloves over to Cyril. 'So — pass these boxes to Gaston; then fill up the sacks. A good night's work, eh Meester Bonhamy?'

'Oh wee,' said Cyril, giving him a ghastly smile. He pulled on the gloves and tried to look tough and wicked. 'Let's go, baby,' he said, putting on an American accent.

It was while lifting boxes off the lower shelves that Cyril noticed a large red button set in the wall behind a small pane of glass. Above was the word *Alarme*.

It was not possible to do anything just then. Michel was working beside him and he could see Gaston's piggy eyes fixed on him from time to time. But he managed to conceal the alarm button with one of the empty boxes — which he placed so that its sharp metal corner was against the pane of glass.

Some of the boxes contained papers. But most held jewellery. And Cyril thought he'd never seen such marvellous things — rings with emeralds as big as golf balls, gold bracelets it was quite difficult to lift; in one box, a handful of large, loose diamonds. Despite himself, Cyril rather enjoyed filling his sack. He put in a pearl necklace he knew Deirdre would like. There was a jewelled fountain pen he quite fancied himself.

After two hours they'd filled six sacks. 'Enough!' cried Pierre. 'We can carry no more. Now we celebrate.'

He reached for the wicker case from the hotel and took out three bottles of champagne. They drank from gold goblets that Pierre took from the top of his sack.

Cyril felt he could really do with some champagne. He was still spattered with la sewarge and had been exhausted by the long night's work. He was also frightened by what was going on.

After three goblets he felt a good deal better. He took a fourth and then stood up and lazily strolled to the side of the bank vault as though he'd seen something interesting. The three robbers were talking excitedly in French, waving their arms and drinking.

Cyril took a quick look to make sure he was not

being watched, and then bent sharply forward, shoving his bottom as hard as he could against the metal box he'd put so that its edge was touching the glass of the *Alarme* button.

At once — pandemonium. Through the thick steel door they could hear the muffled sound of a siren set off in the bank outside. But immediately afterwards they were deafened by a dreadful clanging in the vault itself.

'We 'ave been discovered,' cried Pierre, leaping to his feet. He shouted orders in French, and Gaston slid down the rope to the sewer below. Michel passed the sacks down and then slid after him.

'Queeck, Mr Bonhamy,' shouted Pierre, standing by the light switch, 'go down. Down.'

With some difficulty, Cyril managed to half fall, half slide through the floor; followed moments later by Pierre.

The sacks were so heavy that although, after the first few steps, Cyril had hurriedly emptied half of his into the sewer, he could still only just carry it. Fortunately this meant that Gaston and Michel, who carried two sacks each, could go no faster than a rapid walk. Pierre, carrying one sack so that he could also read the map, led the way. Cyril tottered along in the rear.

After fifteen minutes Pierre stopped and held up his hand. They listened, and suddenly Cyril heard from far behind them, echoing down the long dark sewers, the faint but sinister sound of dogs barking. It was the gendarmes — with hounds.

Pierre immediately jumped into a fairly shallow sewer which led off to the right and went splashing up it.

'We throw them off the scent,' he shouted.

Too tired to argue, Cyril sploshed after them. 'I might as well get covered in the stuff,' he thought wearily.

But ten minutes later they were in still worse trouble. Pierre was leading them on a narrow path beside one of the long, straight, main sewers, when once again he stopped and held up his hand. They listened carefully. Cyril could just hear the hounds, much fainter behind them. And then he heard what had stopped Pierre: from somewhere not far in front the sound of singing.

They were trapped! Behind, the gendarmes. In front, a gang of men singing. No doubt the sewer workmen arriving to start their horrid day's work.

But not for nothing was Pierre Melon the most wanted man in France. Flashing his torch across the sewer he saw the round black opening of a side tunnel.

'Queeck,' he called. 'We escape up 'ere.'

The main sewer was about six feet wide. Pierre cleared it with a single bound and then crouched in the tunnel opening while Gaston threw the sacks across one by one. Next Gaston jumped across. Then Michel.

'Jump, Cyril,' called Pierre. 'Queeck — you must jump now. I catch you.'

'I can't,' shouted Cyril, looking with distaste at

the six-foot-wide sluggish black river glistening in the light from his torch. 'Je rest ici. Leave me to mon fate. Or revoir.'

But it wasn't just that he couldn't. He suddenly realized he shouldn't be running away from the gendarmes. He should have been running towards them. He would explain his perfectly natural mistake about le Beebles. About how he had been forced to take part in the robbery, and how he had pressed the alarm. He would show the gendarmes the tunnel down which Pierre had escaped. There might be a reward.

And then to his horror he saw that Pierre, as though guessing his plans, was waving his revolver at him. 'Don't shoot,' Cyril shouted urgently. 'I'll try and jump. Don't shootez pas.'

But Pierre had grown rather fond of the fat little English criminal. He was shouting in French that he would not desert his friend. If the gendarmes came he would keep them back with his revolver. And just to show he meant what he said, he fired a couple of shots up the sewer in the direction of the now much louder barking of the hounds.

"All right, all right,' cried Cyril, terrified, 'stop shooting. I'm jumping.' Not understanding a word of what Pierre had been shouting, it had simply sounded to Cyril like a stream of fearful threats, followed by an attempt to kill him.

He braced himself against the slimy wall of the sewer, then pushed off with all his force and hurled himself out over the blackness. He was tired, but fear gave him strength. He shot a good distance across the thick black stream and then, some way short of Pierre's reaching hands, fell with a tremendous splash into the very middle.

For a moment he disappeared beneath the surface. But the sewer was only about five feet deep. Cyril struggled to the edge and was pulled up into the tunnel entrance, where he stood, water pouring off him, and very angry indeed.

'Look what you've made me do with your ridiculous shooting,' said Cyril furiously. 'Look at me. Look at la sewarge, for one thing.' But already lights had appeared at the far end of the main sewer they had just left. Pierre grabbed Cyril's hand and pushed him rather roughly forward into the darkness.

Five minutes later they were standing blinking in one of the main streets of Nice. The tunnel had led straight to an iron ladder that went up to a manhole.

The three robbers might just have escaped notice. They might have been three workmen carrying sacks of something. But it was impossible not to notice Cyril. Covered in la sewarge from head to toe, he was black all over. He smelt very strongly indeed. Each step left a large, splodgy footprint.

Although it was only seven-thirty in the morning, and although they tried to hide him in the middle, a good many people did begin to notice Cyril.

Pierre, Michel and Gaston were soon muttering anxiously together. Cyril didn't care. Nothing mattered. He'd decided that if they came anywhere near the Hotel Splendide he'd simply dash inside and yell for Deirdre. He didn't care if Pierre shot at him. He didn't much care what happened.

He was, however, vaguely aware that Pierre and Gaston were working out some plan. When it came, it was a typical Melon plan; daring, dangerous and violent.

A few minutes later, a powerful French car, a large white Mercedes, drew up at the pavement in front of them. As the owner, a strong-looking man with a beard, stepped out, Gaston and Michel flung themselves upon him. There was a short struggle and the man with the beard reeled back over a café table.

They threw the sacks of jewellery into the back of the car, bundled Cyril in on top of them, and moments later they were roaring at top speed through the early morning streets of Nice.

Cyril, crouching down among the sacks, beginning to feel cold as well as disgusting, thought, 'Nothing can be worse than this.'

Unfortunately, as he was to learn over the next few days, he was wrong.

Cyril Tries to Escape

Pierre drove furiously for five hours, hurling the big car round corners so that Cyril was bounced about uncomfortably with the clinking sacks of jewellery.

La sewarge gradually dried until it was a sort of crust all over him. Lumps fell off. Gaston and Michel had climbed over into the front to avoid sitting near him. They kept all the windows open.

At lunch-time Pierre drove into a small mountain village and parked behind a hotel. Cyril waited in the car until they were able to let him in unseen by a back door.

Then at last — while Pierre and the others went shopping — Cyril was able to get out of his filthy clothes and have a bath. In fact he had two baths — letting out the thick black water after the first and starting again.

As soon as he was more or less clean, he wrapped a towel round his middle and padded swiftly out into the hotel corridor.

It took him some time to find the thin woman who seemed to run the place and even longer to get her to show him the telephone. As far as French went she was more or less an idiot. But Cyril managed to keep his temper. He realized the sooner he could telephone Deirdre or the gendarmes the better.

Unfortunately, it had taken so long to get the idiotic woman to understand what he meant that as he was about to use the telephone on the first floor, he saw Pierre in the hall below, returning from the shopping expedition. At once Cyril scampered nervously back to the bathroom.

Pierre had bought toothbrushes, combs, pyjamas, shirts and suits. There were two nice grey suits for each of them. For the robbers, in case the owner of the white Mercedes had passed on their description. For Cyril because his clothes had been completely ruined by la sewarge. They had also bought four suitcases.

While he was dressing, Cyril planned his next move. As he had been prevented from telephoning just then, the sooner he tried again the better. In fact, best of all would be to escape altogether. Pierre was the dangerous one. It was clear that he had already guessed roughly what Cyril would do. The fact that he had tried to shoot him showed how dangerous he was. But he was also very cunning.

He still treated Cyril with great politeness. Cyril wasn't fooled for an instant.

When they were all dressed in their new clothes, Pierre called them together and explained what they would do. They would drive north to the town of Charleville, just on the Belgian border. Once over the border, they would go to one of Pierre's most secret hideouts, where they would be safe.

Not just safe. 'And there we 'ave les girls,' cried Pierre. 'Eh, Bonhamy? You like ze girls — no?'

Cyril thought of Deirdre. Deirdre wasn't exactly a girl, but he certainly wanted to see her at that moment. However, he had to play Pierre's little game. 'Oh wee, les girls,' said Cyril winking. 'Oh, la la! Oh Can-can! Frou-frou! Wee!'

But at this point Gaston suddenly spoke. 'Why do we 'ave to take heem?' he said, pointing a thick finger at Cyril. 'Why we not leeve heem on 'is own?'

'Well, I certainly don't want to be a burden,' began Cyril. But Pierre interrupted.

'No no no,' he said quickly. 'Our friend Bonhamy is one of us. We look after heem.'

But Gaston, still staring at Cyril with his piggy eyes, now had another idea. 'Perhaps you theenk he plan to go to the gendarmes?' he said slowly. 'You theenk he want the reward — eh?'

'Don't be a fool, Gaston,' said Pierre, laughing as if the idea were ridiculous. 'Monsieur Bonhamy 'ave no more weesh to 'ave the gendarmes than we do — eh?'

However, Gaston simply couldn't believe that Cyril was a famous English criminal. From that moment on, he decided to watch him very carefully indeed.

While they were shopping, Michel had stolen some number plates off a car. He and Gaston now went to fix these on the Mercedes. Pierre, meanwhile, gave Cyril two more things he'd bought for him — a large tin of Elastoplast and some sheets of stiff white paper. 'That's very kind of you,' said Cyril, puzzled. 'But what . . . where . . . how . . .?' He waved the paper helplessly at Pierre.

Once again, Pierre was amazed at Cyril's courage. 'Even now you would face the world without your disguise,' he cried. '*C'est magnifique.* But I do not theenk it ees wise, my friend. Pleese — permit me.' And to Cyril's horror — though he was far too frightened of the French criminal to object — Pierre began to cut something that looked like a large white beak out of the paper.

When it was fixed over Cyril's nose with the Elastoplast he could hardly see round it. What he could see, in the hotel mirror, looked like a mixture between Concorde and something in a circus.

All that afternoon they roared north in the big Mercedes. The sacks of jewellery had been locked in the boot. Gaston and Michel sat on the large front seat, taking it in turns with Pierre to drive. Cyril had the back seat to himself, apart from the cases.

He had planned to watch the route so that if he

had a chance — a moment alone with a waiter, even a telephone — he could get word to the gendarmes. But he hadn't been to bed at all the night before. The whole sewarge business had been absolutely exhausting. Five minutes after they'd started, Cyril had fallen into a deep sleep.

He woke when they arrived in the late evening at another secluded hotel on the outskirts of some little town.

Supper was rather jolly. Pierre as usual ordered champagne. Although it was difficult either to eat or drink in his beak, Cyril managed to have several glasses. He began to feel much better. Somehow he'd escape or get word to the gendarmes.

And after a while he found that Pierre enjoyed talking about books. At first, he kept asking about Madam Big until Cyril said irritably, 'Why do you keep asking about her? She was nothing.' At which Pierre said in astonishment, 'Nothing?' Then, turning to Gaston, he said, 'Did you 'ear that, my friend?'

Gaston just grunted. He didn't believe Cyril had had anything to do with Madam Big. He wanted revenge for his nose, and for the way Cyril had come crashing down on top of him in the sewer.

After supper they went to their rooms. While he waited for the robbers to fall asleep, Cyril wrote notes on the hotel paper. Since the newspapers would be full of the robbery, he realized the mere mention of Pierre's name would send people rushing to the gendarmes. He had almost given up confidence in the French being able to speak their own language so he wrote the messages in simple English:

MELON IS HERE. MELON GOING TO CHARLEVILLE.

He'd learnt the new car number off by heart and wrote that down:

> MELON — CAR NUMBER 1009 BS 83. MELON HERE — TELL GENDARMES.

At half-past ten he slipped out of his door and tip-toed down the corridor. He was getting inside a telephone box by Reception when he felt a heavy hand on his shoulder.

It was Gaston. 'What are you doing weeth telephone?' he asked suspiciously.

'I am phoning my wife,' said Cyril coldly. 'She will be worried. I trust you will allow me to do that?'

'You weel not tell 'er where we are or where we go?' said Gaston.

'Of course not,' said Cyril, who had planned to do just that.

It took some time to get through to the Hotel Splendide, and almost as long to get Deirdre. They still seemed to be down as Monsieur and Madame Pomme de Terre. Things weren't made easier by Gaston, who had his foot and head well inside the door of the telephone box.

Eventually, however, he heard the sleepy voice of his wife.

'It's me, Deirdre. Cyril.'

'Cyril! Where are you? Oh — I've been so worried.'

'No need to worry, darling,' said Cyril. 'I'm with my Beeble friends.' He stopped, trying to think how he could explain to her what was going on. 'Not,' he said.

'Not?' said Deirdre. 'Not what? Cyril — are you all right?'

'No,' said Cyril. 'Frightful. Beeble friends not.' And then, struck by a sudden idea, he said, 'Dangerous fruit — Beeble friends not — with frightful fruit.'

'Are you ill, Cyril?' cried Deirdre. He sounded quite mad. She suddenly thought, He's probably got sunstroke, he's wandering about in a high fever, raving.

'Dangerous fruit frightful Beeble friends not,' babbled Cyril again desperately.

But Deirdre interrupted. 'Cyril, are you still wearing your nose cover?' she asked in a worried voice.

'I most certainly am,' said Cyril, suddenly made irritable. How could Deirdre ask about his nose at this vital moment? He was sick of people bothering about his nose cover. Why couldn't they leave his nose alone? 'If you're really interested, I look a complete idiot,' he said.

But now Gaston was pulling him roughly by the

shoulder. Cyril just had time to say rapidly, 'Well, I've got to fly, darling — frightful Beeble fruit dangerous friends not,' and he was yanked from the phone box.

Outside, he shook Gaston's heavy hand from his shoulder and walked angrily towards his room again. He wasn't at all sure he'd got his message clearly across to Deirdre. It was entirely Gaston's fault. In fact, he was so cross and also worried that he walked straight into the wrong room. It was the one next to his own. He'd slammed the door and turned on the light before he realized his mistake.

He was in what was really a large cupboard. It seemed to be the place where the chamber-maids hung their clothes and uniforms. Aprons, overalls, black skirts and frilly caps hung on hooks along the wall; there were even black tights and some high-heeled shoes. Cyril quickly stuffed some of these into a large plastic bag. He had no clear plan, but if things got more desperate they might come in useful.

When he came out of the cupboard he saw Gaston's door whip open. He ignored it entirely and simply strode into his own room, once again slamming the door behind him.

Twice more he tried to get out of his room and back to the telephone. Each time Gaston's door opposite flew open. Cyril realized he was virtually a prisoner.

In the end he rang through to Reception and ordered twenty-four bottles of Coca-Cola. He emptied these out of the window and in each empty bottle he put one of his messages. He realized it was no good just leaving pieces of paper lying about. They'd be ignored, blown away or swept up. Besides, he'd have to throw messages at gendarmes and through gendarme station windows. And he knew no one could resist reading a message in a bottle.

It was after two o'clock when Cyril had filled all the bottles with messages and packed them, together with the various bits and pieces of chamber-maid's uniform, into his case. He also filled his pockets with messages. He fell exhausted into bed and was soon asleep.

Next morning he left a bottle with a message down his bed. He threw another into the maids' cupboard on his way down. And in the hall he pressed a message hurriedly into the hands of one of the maids.

When they'd left, one of her friends called across.

'Did he give you much then, Marie?'

'Not on your life,' Marie called back. ' 'E must be mad. Some note about melons,' and she threw Cyril's message disgustedly into a waste-paper basket.

They drove north all morning. Cyril sat in the back beside the open window. Every now and again he reached into the case beside him and, taking care the others didn't see, threw a bottle out of the window.

He threw them at shop windows, into cafés and

the backs of lorries. He tossed them over bridges into rivers, and when they stopped for petrol he left a bottle prominently in the toilet and dropped two more out of the window as they drove off.

By lunch-time he had used up most of his bottles and there still didn't seem to be any pursuit. Cyril couldn't understand it. He felt France was littered with bottles.

While Pierre and the other two were having coffee, Cyril walked casually out of the dining room, hoping to find a telephone. But Gaston followed him and he had to pretend he was just wandering about having a look at things. However, he'd brought a bottle from the car concealed in his coat and he managed to drop it into an ice bucket on their way out.

He'd finished all his bottles by the middle of the afternoon. After that he lay slumped in the back of the big Mercedes while Pierre drove north at a ridiculous and dangerous speed. Whenever they stopped at traffic lights or in a traffic jam Cyril wondered if he ought to make a dash for it. But he knew quite well they would easily catch him. Pierre would probably just wind down the window and shoot him.

By the time they reached their hotel that evening in the little town of Longeau, Cyril was becoming extremely worried. Pierre said they would get to Charleville the next day.

'Tomorrow night we cross the border into

Belgium — and we are safe,' he called cheerfully. 'How do you say to that, my friend?'

'Oh, marvellous,' said Cyril gloomily from the back of the car.

It suddenly seemed possible he might never escape from the robbers. He might have to spend years floundering about in sewers robbing banks and wearing huge pieces of paper over his nose. Eventually they'd be caught and he'd spend the rest of his life in prison.

They had champagne for supper as usual. The owner of the hotel was a very big Frenchman with a red face and a beard called Monsieur Jacques. He was sitting at the next table singing songs and drinking large glasses of wine.

Pierre called their waitress and had two bottles of champagne sent over as a present. *'À votre santé,'* he shouted, raising his glass.

Cyril thought this was a mistake. He'd already seen Monsieur Jacques drink three bottles of red wine and goodness knows how much he'd had before. Every time a waitress passed his table he tried to grab hold of her. He might well get violent.

What happened was that Monsieur Jacques got noisier than ever. Cyril had ordered fifty-six bottles of Coca-Cola to be sent up to his room. Emptying them into the basin, he could hear the songs being bellowed round the dining room below. After a while he heard what sounded like furniture and bottles being smashed. 'No one will be able to sleep while this goes on,' he thought irritably, while writing out messages and stuffing them into the bottles.

And in fact each time he very quietly opened his door and tried to slip out, Gaston, who had once again managed to get the room opposite him, opened his own door and stuck his head out.

Finally, at one-thirty, there was silence from downstairs. But Gaston was still watching. When, after waiting ten minutes, Cyril poked his head out of his door, the door opposite once again sprang open.

There seemed nothing for it but to try out the plan he'd vaguely thought of the night before.

Cyril wouldn't have done it had he not been desperate. He was not very good at acting. In particular, he didn't think he was much good at acting as a woman. Also, the chamber-maid's clothes he'd collected the night before looked rather small.

However, he was surprised and pleased to find they were quite a good fit. The frilly cap came all round his head and could be tied to cover most of his face. A tight black skirt, pretty black blouse and a pair of long black tights all fitted fairly well. Only the high-heeled shoes weren't much good — they'd come from different pairs, one too tight and one too loose. Walking was rather difficult.

Cyril picked up one of the trays on which his Coca-Cola had arrived and tip-toed to the door. He listened a moment, then opened it, stepped quickly out and turned round so that his back was towards Gaston.

At the same time he said in a high, squeaky, woman's voice, 'Bon night, m'sieur, bon night', pulled the door shut and wobbled as fast as he could down the corridor.

He could almost feel Gaston's eyes staring at his back, but there was no pursuit. Just not wearing that silly paper nose makes it impossible for him to recognize me, thought Cyril.

All was silent and fairly dark downstairs, though a number of broken bottles showed the signs of Monsieur Jacques's earlier jollities. Cyril wobbled as quickly as he could across the hall and out through the revolving door.

The steep little street was empty, lit by a bright moon. Cyril hurried up it as fast as the hill and his high heels allowed him. If he saw a gendarme or the gendarme station he'd stop. Otherwise he'd just keep going all night. He wanted to get as far away from Gaston, Pierre and Michel as he possibly could.

However, he had to stop and rest at the top of the hill. He was out of breath and his feet were torture. He couldn't understand why women wore high-heeled shoes — or how.

He was teetering painfully down the next street when he saw someone coming towards him in the moonlight.

It was someone large and singing. A man. He was either ill or drunk, because he lurched from side to side and twice fell down.

As he drew near, Cyril saw to his horror that it

was Monsieur Jacques — now clearly very drunk indeed. He was carrying a bottle of something from which every now and again he took a large swig.

Cyril stepped into the road to avoid the hotel owner. Perhaps he would be too drunk to notice him.

But as they drew level, Monsieur Jacques lurched into the road and stood swaying in front of Cyril. 'Blah blah blah blah,' he said in drunken French, impossible to understand. 'Blah blah blah.'

'Pas tonight, merci beaucoup,' squeaked Cyril daintily. 'Je have to aller home to my maman, merci thank you.'

The hotel owner belched and, leaning forward, made a grab at Cyril.

'Ma maman,' squeaked Cyril, stepping back. 'Elle est très worried about her petite daughter.'

'Blah blah blah,' said Monsieur Jacques. He opened both his arms and advanced unsteadily towards Cyril.

It was obviously no good arguing. Cyril turned round and started up the street again as fast as he could in his high-heeled shoes.

But this appeared to excite Monsieur Jacques further. Cyril heard six or seven loud belches and then, terrifyingly, the sound of thudding feet as the hotel owner started to run.

Cyril reached the corner a few steps in front. He pulled his skirt high above his knees and, without even pausing to pull off the by now agonising high-heeled shoes, simply flew down the steep cobbled street back towards the hotel.

Somehow or other he managed to keep his feet. The same was not true of Monsieur Jacques. Cyril heard roars of pain and fearful crashes from behind him. It sounded as if the hotel owner was rolling down the hill with a lot of dustbins.

Cyril himself was quite unable to stop. He struck the revolving door with great force, was whirled violently round, and flung into the hotel face down across the hall. He scrambled to his feet, wobbled at high speed up the stairs, and dashed back down his corridor. Behind him he heard another tremendous smashing noise as Monsieur Jacques seemed to crash straight into the hotel, bringing the whole revolving door with him.

As Cyril reached his room, Gaston appeared in front of him. Cyril charged into him, sending him flying, pulled open the door of his own room, almost fell in, locked the door and collapsed on his bed.

It took him ten minutes to recover enough to take off his chamber-maid's clothes and get into bed. As he fell asleep, he heard Gaston shouting something and shaking his door.

In the distance there were sounds of clinking and songs being sung. Monsieur Jacques had started his party again.

Cyril Escapes!

Cyril could hardly walk the next morning. He was also covered in bruises. But he realized as he hobbled down to the dining room that today was his last chance of escaping. By evening they'd be at Pierre's hideout in Belgium and goodness knows how he'd get out of that.

At breakfast he had the first bit of good news since he'd bumped into Pierre in the Hotel Splendide. Michel was sick.

' 'Ee 'ave la grippe — 'ow you say? The colly-wobbles. So — for one day we stay 'ere. We stay quiet in our rooms — 'ow you say? — lie doggy.'

Pierre was in a playful mood, despite the setback.

'Gaston is telling me you are 'aving saucy leetle chamber-maid in your room, eh?' he said, giving Cyril a playful biff. 'I am afraid it 'ees one more day

54

you 'ave to wait — then I promise you les girls. Ow you say to that, eh?'

'Oh la la,' said Cyril testily, managing to avoid another of Pierre's irritating nudges.

He had no intention at all of lying doggy — whatever that meant. This was his chance and he intended taking it.

He waited ten minutes in his room after breakfast, then gently opened his door.

At once, to his extreme annoyance, Gaston's head shot out from the room opposite. This happened three times.

Cyril next tried his window. But the drop into the street was at least twenty feet, straight on to hard cobbles. Wearily he drew in his head. There was nothing for it — it would have to be the chamber-maid's uniform again.

There was a tear in the pretty black blouse, and a stain on the tight black skirt. But Cyril managed to make himself look more or less respectable with some safety pins. He tied the frilly cap tight across his face and forced his feet into the high-heeled shoes.

He didn't even bother to pack, but just stripped the sheets off his bed and walked out of his room with them piled in a great bundle in his arms.

Gaston may have been surprised to see a chamber-maid suddenly pop out of Cyril's room; or he may have just thought the Englishman was up to his 'saucy tricks' again. In any case, he didn't bother to follow.

Cyril wobbled painfully down the corridor and then still more painfully down the stairs into the hallway. Here he dropped the sheets and prepared to make his escape.

The hall was still in quite a mess. The revolving door had been bashed off entirely. Unfortunately Cyril's passage through the broken bottles and bits of smashed door coincided with the arrival from somewhere in the back of the hotel of Monsieur Jacques.

He was feeling absolutely terrible. Covered in cuts and bruises from the dustbins, his huge red face above the beard felt on fire. Every now and again an enormous painful belch blew up in his stomach.

Seeing one of his chamber-maids, he shouted angrily, *'Où est mon café?'*

Cyril pretended not to hear. He'd had quite enough of the hotel owner the night before. He was almost at the opening where the door had been. He could see the street, the sun, the freedom.

The sight of one of his chamber-maids apparently running away made Monsieur Jacques instantly furious. 'XO%!X£!!?' he roared. *'VENEZ ICI! XO&%@Z$O!'*

Cyril decided that perhaps he ought to hear after all. He'd only just got away from Jacques in the darkness. He certainly didn't fancy his chances in broad daylight and still hampered by badly fitting high-heeled shoes.

He stopped and tried to curtsy. 'Wee?' he squeaked sweetly. 'Wee? Que weesh vous, eh?'

The six other maids standing in a trembling line in the dining room trembled still more as they heard Monsieur Jacques yelling at Cyril in the hall. They knew the hotel owner in these moods and he could be most unpleasant.

When he came in some moments later, more or less carrying the new chamber-maid by the scruff of the neck, they could tell that this was one of the worst moods they had ever seen. Monsieur Jacques's face looked like an enormous mad tomato. He had almost finished inspecting their hands when, with a great rumbling and bubbling, he gave one of his colossal belches. Dulcine, a sweet, frail little thing of nineteen, in front of him at the time, almost fainted.

For Cyril the morning passed like some appalling nightmare. He was chased here and shouted at there. No sooner had he finished sweeping up the broken glass in the hallway than he was laying fifty places in the dining room. There were potatoes to peel, then a six-foot-high pile of plates to be washed. Each time, thinking no one was looking, he tried to tip-toe away, Monsieur Jacques would lurch into view and yell at him.

The other maids were most sympathethic to him — particularly the fragile Dulcine.

'*Quelle est votre nom?*' she whispered, pausing by an extremely hot Cyril as he tried to iron what seemed like five hundred napkins.

'Mon nom?' squeaked Cyril in his special chamber-maid's voice. What was his nom? 'Ar —

um — wee,' he squeaked. He couldn't think of anything. At last, as Dulcine was still looking at him, he said, making it as French as he could, 'Deear*dree*. Mon nom is — est — *Dee*ard*ree*.'

'*Comment?*' asked Dulcine, looking a bit puzzled.

'Areee,' squeaked Cyril rather wildly. 'Wee wee — Aree, Furree, Ree-Ree.'

Dulcine put her soft little hand on his shoulder. '*Courage,*' she whispered.

It wasn't until nearly lunch-time that Cyril finally managed to escape to his room. By that time Monsieur Jacques, who had started on the brandy, had lost interest in him and was pursuing the petite Dulcine herself.

Thankful to be in his own clothes again, Cyril sat on his bed with one foot in a basin of water. It had gone quite numb from the high-heeled shoe that was too tight.

Shortly afterwards Pierre came in and said they were going down to lunch. Cyril felt rather nervous going into the dining room again. He almost expected to be recognized. And he was still more nervous when he saw that it was the delicate Dulcine who was waiting on them. But the lovely girl showed no sign of knowing him. And luckily the unpleasant Mr Jacques seemed to have disappeared.

Cyril was rather ashamed to see large burn marks in the shape of an iron on all the napkins. But Pierre ordered champagne as usual, which made him cheer up.

Gloom returned when he was back in his room. He wondered whether he could knot his sheets together, as he had that terrible time when he had been kidnapped by the Arabs, and slide down into the street. But then he saw his sheets were gone. He didn't think a rope made of knotted blankets would really be very safe.

However, it was leaning out of his window that he suddenly saw his first real chance to escape. At the far end of the cobbled street a large cart with high wooden sides pulled by an old horse was slowly coming towards the hotel. Sitting behind the horse a very old man nodded, holding the reins loosely in his hands. And piled even above the high wooden sides was what looked like a load of rather dark hay, the top of which reached not far below the first-floor windows.

Trembling with excitement and fear, Cyril grabbed his case and scrambled up on to the window sill.

Nearer and nearer rumbled the cart, its huge load gently swaying. Cyril hardly dared look. Nearer and nearer — two houses away, now one, now directly underneath. His eyes shut, holding his breath, Cyril launched himself into space.

Perhaps it would have been better if he had dared look. As it was, he shot down about six feet and then, with a noise between a *plop!* and a *squelch!* vanished almost up to his neck in what the cart was carrying.

It wasn't a load of hay at all but a load of — what?

Hot, damp, squelchy — it was just another lot of la sewarge, which you seemed to find all over France. Gasping and panting, with much mulching and squelching, Cyril struggled out of it and eventually managed to get right up on top and sit on the edge.

But then, despite the smell, the bits of straw and this and that, he did suddenly begin to feel much better. The cart trundled slowly through the narrow streets of Longeau. Soon they were out in the open countryside and the hotel was left behind, and with it Gaston, Michel and Pierre.

For a while the cart followed the main road. Then the horse turned down a little lane and went plodding along between green fields and high grassy banks.

'I'm free!' thought Cyril. 'I've done it. I've escaped!'

For some time nothing else mattered. But after a while he realized it wasn't really at all pleasant on top of the cart. Besides, he didn't want to be carried too far from the main road. They happened to be passing between two particularly high banks at that moment and it was fairly simple to climb off on to one of these as they brushed past.

Cyril watched the cart lumber away from him. He felt very grateful and thought perhaps he should thank the kind old man who, without knowing it, had helped him escape. On the other hand, he didn't want to startle the old fellow. And looking as he did at that moment, Cyril realized he would have startled anyone.

The first thing to do was clean himself up. He could see from his bank that a little stream ran along the bottom of the field below him.

He hurried down to it and after a lot of painful splashing about in freezing water looked a good deal better. His clothes were far too thickly covered to get clean so he threw them away and put on the second light grey suit Pierre had thoughtfully provided. He combed his hair, scrubbed his shoes with grass, and set off to return to the main road again.

It was still the middle of the afternoon and the sun shone in a cloudless sky. Cyril was exhausted after his morning's work as a maid. His case grew heavier and heavier and he was tempted to throw that away too. In the end he threw away all but one of the fifty-six Coca-Cola bottles filled with messages. He decided to keep one so that he could show the gendarmes how he had tried to contact them, if they still hadn't found a bottle when he telephoned them.

At the main road he turned left, away from Longeau. He didn't know where it led to and he didn't care. All he wanted was a telephone. A quick call to the local gendarmes and those evil men would be seized and clapped into gaol.

At first Cyril hurried off the road every time he heard a car coming behind him. But he soon realized this was pointless. Michel was ill, and he himself was now some miles from Longeau. Indeed, rather than avoid cars, it would be more sensible to stop them.

The road was long and had also started to go uphill. The sun was hot. Cyril passed his suitcase from one hand to the other.

French drivers seemed no more able to understand simple hitch-hiking signals than they could their own language. As car after car whizzed past him without stopping, Cyril grew increasingly irritated. Finally, at the end of a particularly long, hot, straight stretch of road he decided to plonk himself more or less in front of the next car that came. It would either have to stop or run him over.

For a long time nothing came. Cyril stood staring back into the distance, shading his eyes from the sun.

And then, at long last, he heard a distant hum. Shortly afterwards he saw a little dot moving along the valley below him. He stepped out into the middle of the road.

The car was coming very fast. He could hear it approaching and soon, a cloud of dust swirling behind, it appeared at the end of the long stretch of road he had just covered.

For some reason it looked oddly familiar. Cyril peered into the sun, waving his arm vigorously. Was the car white? He shaded his eyes again, and looked out anxiously, waving his other arm more and more slowly. Surely, he thought with a sinking heart, surely it couldn't be a white Mercedes that was speeding towards him on the road from Longeau?

It could be and it was. Seconds later he was

staring in horror at three far too familiar faces, faces he had hoped never to see again, except perhaps behind bars.

It was Pierre who spoke first.

'Ah, ah, my friend,' he said, smiling, 'thees ees indeed a piece of luck.'

In Deadly Danger

At first Cyril thought he might faint or be extremely sick. Then he wondered if he dare make a dash for it — over the fields and away.

But after a few seconds he managed to force a ghastly smile across his face.

'Thank goodness you've come,' he said. 'But not luck. Oh no — I expected it. Planned it. Part of my plan.'

'So — you knew about les gendarmes?' cried Pierre.

'Of course,' said Cyril, wondering what on earth Pierre was talking about. 'Didn't you get my message? I left a note with the maid, Dulcine.'

'And so it was you, my brave friend, 'oo create — 'ow you say? — a decoy? A diversion? 'Oo draw them away?' Pierre was beaming.

'Exactly,' said Cyril. 'Easy as anything. A few

telephone calls, some quick thinking, then my getaway — a horse and cart.'

Pierre turned and spoke rapidly to Gaston, who simply shrugged his shoulders and spat out of the window.

'Our friend Gaston 'ere, 'ee theenk you betray us,' Pierre said to Cyril, laughing. 'I tell 'eem 'ee ees wrong. But now I say — eet ees Monsieur Bonhamy 'oo save us.'

'Exactly,' said Cyril.

He learnt roughly what had happened as they drove on towards Charleville. During the afternoon, four gendarmes had suddenly turned up at the hotel. Michel had spotted them on one of his frequent visits to the bathroom.

He had alerted the others, who had been very worried to find Cyril and his suitcase gone. Gaston had at once said it was Cyril who had given them away.

Then, to their surprise and delight, the gendarmes had as suddenly left. The three robbers had wondered whether to stay on at the hotel, but had decided it was too dangerous. Besides, Pierre had said, Mr Bonhamy can look after himself.

' 'Ee can look after 'imself, that one, I say,' said Pierre. 'And now we find it ees you 'oo is 'aving saved us!'

Cyril listened gloomily in the back of the car. To have been free, to have escaped, and then to be caught again was bad enough. But to learn that if he had only stayed put he could almost certainly have found a way of altering the gendarmes made it even worse.

They stopped for supper at a small restaurant. Before they got out Pierre turned round and shook his finger at Cyril.

'Ah, my friend,' he said, 'always eet ees the same. You are too brave, too bold. You forget the disguise.' And to Cyril's irritation he handed over another long beak of white paper.

I might as well be married to him, thought Cyril crossly.

Pierre decided they shouldn't sleep in a hotel and they spent an extremely uncomfortable night in the Mercedes.

It was especially uncomfortable for Cyril. He shared the back seat with Michel, whose collywobbles seemed worse, if anything. He spent most of the night groaning and clambering in and out of the car. Cyril hardly slept a wink.

And in the morning, terror took the place of gloom. As they roared steadily north it began to seem impossible that he could escape being taken over the border and shut up for ever in Pierre's dreaded hideout.

But in the end it was Gaston who gave them away.

They had stopped in some large town for petrol and, instead of following Cyril as he usually did, Gaston had wandered off on his own. Cyril had decided that this was his chance to leave his last bottle and was searching around for a really obvious place when he heard shots and the sound of men shouting.

The next instant Gaston appeared, running as fast as he could towards the petrol station. Behind him ran a gendarme. As he ran, Gaston turned and fired at the gendarme, who threw himself flat and fired back.

Now Pierre was shouting, 'Queek — Meester Bonhamy — we go — queek! queek!'

Cyril, who had suddenly seen a way to escape by running up to the gendarme, changed his mind. Pierre was waving his revolver about in a thoroughly dangerous way. So instead of escaping, Cyril hurled his precious last bottle in the direction of the gendarme and ran over to the Mercedes.

Gaston jumped into the front, Pierre fired at the gendarme, Cyril scrambled into the back — and they were away.

As they left, the gendarme ran up to the garage, seized a big car that had been filled at the pump behind them and roared off in pursuit.

The gendarme had taken a Citroën. It was about as fast as the Mercedes and at first it looked as though they might be caught. Pierre screeched round corners and drove recklessly up one-way streets. Gaston and Michel leant out of the window, firing at the gendarme pursuing them.

Cyril lay with his eyes tight shut on the floor of the car. At any moment he expected them to crash or turn over — or explode as the gendarme fired into their petrol tank. Trembling with terror, he piled the suitcases on top of himself for extra protection.

But once they were out into the open country it became clear that Pierre was the better driver. Gradually the gap between the two cars grew wider. Cyril raised his head from the floor and peered cautiously out of the window at the speeding countryside. Finally he pulled himself on to the seat again.

It was really almost fun. Pierre raced along the main road, passing car after car. The Citroën dropped away behind. Then all at once Pierre swerved into a narrow country road to the left. He raced up the steep hill between high banks and at the top turned through a gate into a field and stopped the Mercedes behind the hedge. Pulling Cyril with them, the three robbers crouched down behind the car, revolvers in their hands.

It was peaceful in the little field. Some brown cows munched the green grass. The afternoon sun was warm, but a gentle breeze stopped it becoming too hot. Cyril watched a blue and white butterfly flutter into the open window of the Mercedes and perch on the steering wheel.

It was clear the gendarme hadn't seen them turning off. There was no pursuit. Everyone stood up and stretched. Pierre lit a cigarette. 'You 'elp us like I expect you would,' he said to Cyril. 'I see you throw that bottle at 'eem — eet was magnificent.'

'Oh — it was nothing much,' said Cyril modestly. 'I don't suppose I hit him.'

The three Frenchmen began to gabble together in their bad French. As far as Cyril could follow, Gaston was explaining how the gendarme had almost caught him. Gaston had thought it was time they changed the number plates on the Mercedes again, and he was busy unscrewing the number plates from a parked Ford when the gendarme had appeared on the scene.

'A beet of bad luck, eh, Bonhamy?' Pierre said to Cyril. 'But that gendarme will 'ave our number for sure. We weel 'ave to tak the leetle country roads to Charleville.'

At the mention of Charleville, Cyril felt once more extremely gloomy. He had really quite enjoyed the chase, and had been almost as pleased as Pierre that they had escaped. He'd forgotten it would have been far better for him if they had been caught.

They arrived in the town at five o'clock. Some sort of fair was in progress, and there were posters everywhere and flags across the streets. One of the main attractions was a giant called Olaf Lockjaw. There were posters of him wearing a leopard skin. In some of the pictures he was throwing other wrestlers out of a ring, in others he seemed to be breaking their backs or wringing their necks.

Pierre drove right into the middle of the town, to a hotel called Hotel Orange. It was on the edge of the main square, where the fair was taking place. Giant wheels, dodgems, roundabouts and stalls completely filled it; in the centre was an enormous tent with an eighteen-foot wooden figure of Olaf Lockjaw with a club in his hand standing at the entrance.

But Cyril noticed little of all this. The nearer they'd come to Charleville the more nervous he'd become. As they entered the big, noisy town he began to feel close to panic. If he didn't get away soon he'd never escape.

With his usual cunning, Pierre booked four rooms as if they intended to stay the night. He managed to persuade the hotel to give them a late lunch — or early supper — and ordered champagne.

'To crime!' he said, raising his glass to Cyril.

Cyril didn't answer, but gulped down several tumblers of the bubbly liquid. He was feeling more frightened every minute, but if he were to escape it would require all his courage. He held out his glass. 'More, please,' he said.

After their meal, Pierre said, 'Now, we 'ave one hour sleep — a siesta — then over the border. Just one hour to refresh ourselves, my friends, then — freedom!'

An hour! The time had come to throw caution to the winds. Thanks to the champagne, Cyril felt really quite brave for once — but also cunning. He would alert the hotel, alert the gendarmes, and then flee himself.

Once again, it would mean the chamber-maid's uniform. This was now beginnig to look as though

72

it had been involved in a fight, but Cyril had no other disguise. He pinned it round him as best he could. 'At least it's for the last time,' he thought, cramming his foot into a high-heeled shoe.

He then waited ten minutes, in order to let the robbers fall properly asleep. At last, trembling with fear and excitement he opened his door and slipped out.

All might have been well but for one thing. Hearing Cyril's door open, Gaston sprang to investigate. Seeing only the back of some chamber-maid, he was about to return to his bed, when the chamber-maid turned.

In his excitement Cyril had forgotten to remove the paper cover on his nose. This stuck out several inches from the frilly cap drawn tightly round his face, making him look like some huge chamber-maid bird.

Gaston watched in amazement as this strange creature teetered hurriedly away down the corridor. Then, much puzzled, he set off silently in pursuit.

Cyril wasted no time. He tottered into the dining room, where a few people were sitting down to an early supper.

'Silence!' he shouted. 'Melon dans Room Thirty-four. Vite!'

He ran through the dining room, and made for some steep stairs which led down to the kitchens. Half-way down, one of his heels caught on the edge of a step and he rolled and slid painfully down the rest of the way to land in a heap at the bottom.

But nothing could stop Cyril now. He struggled up and yelled at the top of his voice to the astonished cooks, 'Melon dans Room Thirty-four. Vite! Vite! Melon dans Room Thirty-four,' and scrambled as fast as he could up the stairs again.

He ran — or rather part-ran and part-tottered — back through the dining room and into the hall. Here an elegant young man with long golden hair, whose job it was to greet the guests when they arrived at the Hotel Orange, was arranging some flowers.

Cyril grabbed him by the arms and said breathlessly, 'Vite — Melon dans Room Thirty-four — Vite! Vite!'

'Comment?' said the young man politely.

'Melon,' Cyril said, 'le terrible Melon dans Room Thirty-four.'

But when the young man still stared at him blankly, Cyril turned and ran across to a telephone under a large plastic dome hung at one side of the hall. The only thing was to alert the gendarmes himself — and then get out. And the quickest way to do both was to get Deirdre on to the gendarmes while he fled.

Conversation with the Hotel Splendide was difficult. The line was faint and crackly. And it was some time before Cyril suddenly remembered they were not called Bonhamy.

'What I mean,' he said, 'is I weesh — Je weesh — to parler avec Madame Pomme de Terre — and vite, please, vite.'

And then, at last, there was Deirdre's sensible voice. 'Hullo? Yes? Who is it?'

'Me, Deirdre,' said Cyril. 'Listen, I'm in terrible trouble — you've got to help —'

'Cyril!' interrupted Deirdre. 'Oh, Cyril — where are you? What's happening? Are you all right?'

'No, I'm not all right,' said Cyril. 'Listen. You know that robbery, don't you? Well Melon, the robber, Pierre Melon, is at the Hotel Orange in Charleville — tell the gendarmes *at once* Melon at Hotel Orange — at once . . .'

'What? What?' said Deirdre. 'Don't go so fast. I can't follow. What robbery? Did you say Pierre Orange the robber is at the Hotel Melon . . .'

'For goodness' sake, Deirdre,' cried Cyril, 'this is a matter of life and death. The bank robbery in Nice — in la sewarge — done by Melon *not* Orange. It's *Pierre* Melon, in the *Hotel* Orange in Charleville. Tell the gendarmes at once. Melon in Orange in Charleville — aaaaagh!'

It sounded as if Cyril had suddenly had been stung by a wasp, or even a hornet. Deirdre jumped and held the receiver well away from her ear. Then, putting it nervously back she said, 'Cyril? Cyril? What's happened? Are you all right?'

But there was no answer. The line was dead. They'd been cut off.

Deirdre stood and thought. Melons, oranges, all that fruit — was it just the mad ravings of sunburn again? She wished she asked Cyril about his nose. However, he had mentioned a definite place, Charleville. She picked up the telephone and began to dial a number she now knew by heart, that of the gendarme headquarters in Nice.

Chief Inspector Perriot had been extremely polite and concerned when a tearful Deirdre had told him that her husband had vanished. But there was not much he could do, and all the Nice gendarmes were frantically searching for clues to the bank robbery that had just taken place.

He had been concerned again when she rang him up and told him about the first telephone call. But there was still not much he could do. He agreed, it did sound as if Cyril was a bit unbalanced. He told his men to keep their eyes open for a plump Englishman with a badly sunburnt nose who might be behaving oddly.

But Chief Inspector Perriot was quite different with Deirdre this time.

'What's that?' he said sharply. 'Did you say Pierre Melon? Your 'usband — he speak of a robbery 'ere in Nice?'

'Yes — I'm sorry,' said Deirdre, her voice suddenly breaking as she thought of her poor Cyril still mad as a hatter from sunburn. 'I'm afraid he was as bad as ever — melons, oranges, I couldn't make head or tale of it.'

'No, no, this is not madness at all,' said Chief

Inspector Perriot, pulling a pad towards him. 'Now tell me all that he say, all you can remember.'

They had of course considered Melon among their suspects, since a daring raid through sewers was just the sort of thing he'd have planned. But then a great many of France's top criminals were likely to use the sewers. There were no clues suggesting it was definitely Melon. Besides, Melon had only just escaped from the gendarmes. He wasn't likely to have struck again so soon. There were rumours he'd gone to ground somewhere in Belgium.

But now it seemed it may have been Melon after all. Chief Inspector Perriot smiled grimly when he'd finished speaking to Deirdre. He replaced the telephone receiver and immediately picked it up again. 'Hullo — operator,' he said briskly. 'Get me the chief of the gendarmerie in Charleville. At once.'

Meanwhile, Cyril himself was being carried up the stairs, kicking and struggling, by a triumphant Gaston.

The French robber had lost track of Cyril in his dash through the dining room and down to the kitchen. He'd caught up with him in the hall, just in time to hear the last part of his conversation with Deirdre. He understood quite enough English to realize what Cyril was doing. With a bellow of rage he'd seized Cyril by the neck and yanked him violently away from the telephone.

It had given Cyril the most tremendous fright, and had been quite painful as well. 'Aaaaaagh!' he'd yelled. 'Let go, you horrible man. Put me down at once.'

But struggle as he would, Gaston held him fast. And though it made Cyril very angry, he was also rather worried. It was clear that Gaston was in an ugly mood, a very ugly mood indeed.

The robber carried him along the corridor to Room Thirty-four, knocked at the door, opened it and strode in.

Pierre Melon was standing at the mirror adjusting his black wig over his bald head. He turned in surprise as, pushing Cyril roughly on to the ground, Gaston poured out a stream of angry French.

When he'd finished, Pierre said, 'Ees this true what 'e say, my friend? 'Ee 'ear you telling les gendarmes where it is that I am.' Then looking more closely at the extraordinary figure in front of him, he added, 'And why you wear those very odd clothes, my friend? That skirt? The 'igh 'eels?'

Cyril straightened his frilly cap and tried to pull up the tights. He decided to ignore the first questions, to which he couldn't think of any answer that would really please Pierre. 'These clothes?' he said, smoothing the apron. 'Just a disguise. Like you putting on your wig just now. I thought it best to be safe for our final escape.' He gave another yank to the tights.

Pierre spoke to Gaston, who again poured out a rush of angry French, and then suddenly dashed from the room.

He was back moments later carrying Cyril's suitcase. To Cyril's horror he opened it and tipped the contents on to the floor. Out rolled fifty extra messages which Cyril had scribbled on hotel paper.

Melon read some of those in silence. Then very slowly he looked up and stared at Cyril. Slowly, he smiled.

'So, my friend,' he said very gently. 'So — you prepare messages to tell the gendarmes where I am, eh? You are — 'ow the Eengleesh say? — a clay pigeon.' He took a step towards Cyril.

Cyril took a step back. 'Oh — I'd hardly say that,' he said nervously.

'Oh yes you are, my friend,' said Pierre. He pulled his revolver from inside his jacket and slowly advanced across the room.

Cyril backed away. 'For goodness' sake watch that gun, Mr Melon,' he said nervously. 'We don't want an accident.'

Pierre stopped and raised the gun. 'It will not be an accident, Mr Bonhamy,' he said grimly.

It was at this frightening moment that there came a loud knock at the door.

'Wee,' shouted Cyril. 'Come in. Entrez. Wee.'

The door opened and an elderly waiter appeared. He was carrying a tray on which there was a knife and fork and a huge green melon on a white plate.

'Melon — for Room Thirty-four,' said the waiter.

'Ah wee,' cried Cyril, 'and le vin please — also le beef — le chips — le . . .'

But Pierre interrupted him sharply. He told the waiter to put the melon on the table by the window, between Gaston and Cyril, and then to get out.

Cyril watched in despair while his last chance of rescue shuffled over to the table, put down the tray, bowed and left.

Once more Pierre raised his gun, but this time it was Gaston who stopped him. Standing at the window, he suddenly raised his arms and pointed. '*Regardez,*' he said hoarsely. '*Regardez*, Pierre.'

They all crowded round the window, Cyril now uncomfortably aware of Pierre's gun sticking in his back.

The window of Room Thirty-four looked out into the main square. Although it was still quite light, the fair had already begun. Giant wheels were slowly turning, rocket roundabouts whirling, people were streaming in from all directions, and a spotlight picked out the colossal wooden figure of Olaf Lockjaw.

But it was none of this that had interested Gaston. He had seen a van pull up a hundred yards away at the side of the square. As they watched, grey-uniformed gendarmes poured from its back. Some went one way, some another. But there was no doubt what they were doing. They were surrounding the Hotel Orange.

Pierre wasted no time. He led Gaston and Michel over to the door and gave them hurried orders in French. Then he turned and said quietly, in English, 'I weel follow in a few moments. But first I 'ave to settle a debt of honour — with my leetle clay pigeon 'ere.'

And once again raising his gun, he advanced step by step towards a now really terrified Cyril.

Olaf Lockjaw

'Look, Mr Melon,' said Cyril, backing away towards the window, 'let's not do anything childish. Let's both sit down and talk this over like les grown-ups.'

But it was clear Pierre meant business. He slowly raised his gun and took careful aim at Cyril's heart.

Cyril was not really a man of action, nor was he particularly brave, but he felt so frightened now that he didn't think about anything at all except saving his life.

The high-heeled shoes were different sizes. Cyril suddenly kicked out the foot which had the big one on it. By a lucky chance the shoe shot out and struck Pierre a sharp blow on the side of the head.

At almost the same time Cyril seized the melon

and threw it between Pierre's legs. Then he scrabbled wildly round the room, pulled the door open and dashed out into the corridor.

Leaping forward to stop him, Pierre became entangled with the melon and fell flat on his face. He was up in a moment and, not even bothering to pick up his wig, he raced in pursuit.

Cyril, his skirt gathered up above his waist, galloped lopsidedly down the corridor. He took the stairs to the hall in a single, terrified leap. As he did so he heard the loud crack of Pierre's revolver behind him.

Luckily he landed more or less on top of the delicate young man who had been arranging the flowers. Cyril rolled free, gathered up his skirts again, and raced out into the square. He heard behind him another *crack!* as Pierre fired from the bottom of the stairs.

The gendarmes who had been approaching the Hotel Orange, crouched against the walls, rifles at the ready, broke into a run as they heard the shots. But as the first gendarmes reached the hotel they stopped in astonishment.

Before they could touch the wide double doors, they burst open and an amazing figure shot through them and made — with whirling leaps and limps — straight towards the fair.

It seemed to be one of the hotel chamber-maids. She had one shoe on and one shoe off, one hand held her skirt bunched above the waist, the other tried to hold up sagging tights. An extraordinary cardboard beak, covering most of her face, stuck out of her frilly cap.

But close behind came the man whose bald head was the most recognizable and most wanted in all of France — the terrible Pierre Melon himself. One of the gendarmes started forward with a cry. Another even had time to raise his rifle — but before he could fire, the two figures had vanished into the crowds filling the square. At once the gendarmes set off in pursuit.

Cyril thrust his way through desperately. He gained a brief advantage when some dodgems began moving just after he'd skipped through them, so that Pierre had to go round the outside.

But then Pierre nearly caught Cyril hiding in a tiny roundabout for four-year-olds. He had actually raised his revolver to fire when, luckily, he was knocked on the head by a fire engine with a tinkling bell.

It was at that moment that Cyril saw the opening to the vast tent which had the wooden figure of Olaf Lockjaw outside it. Without pausing, he dashed in.

Olaf Lockjaw boasted that he was the strongest man in the world. An eight-foot-tall, bearded and hairy Swede, he had never been beaten in the wrestling ring. His show was the most exciting and the most popular in the whole fair. He'd challenged anyone to last two minutes in the ring with him. So far the record had been twelve seconds.

The tent was packed with cheering people. Cyril

pushed his way through them. He was too out of breath even to say 'excuse moi'. Sometimes he found it quicker to get on his hands and knees and scrabble his way through legs. That way, too, he could hide from Pierre. But whenever he stood up, or was pulled up, the bald head of his pursuer was always close behind.

It took Cyril seven minutes to fight his way to the middle of the crowd. By then his back was pressed right against the ring. He could see twenty feet — no, fifteen feet away — the figure of Pierre pushing towards him.

There was no escape. With a groan, Cyril turned and — hampered by his skirt and tights and apron and single, very tight, high-heeled shoe — he began to clamber into the ring.

At that moment there came the sound of a loudspeaker. *'Attention! Attention!'* it boomed. *'Silence, s'il vous plaît! Attention!'*

It was the gendarmes. Pierre stopped his chase for an instant and looked back to the big main door of the tent.

The entrance was swarming with armed gendarmes. Even as he watched, they began to force their way into the tight-packed crowd. Although no one was taking much notice, Pierre realized it was some sort of announcement about himself. He could just make out references to baldness and scars, and the words Melon and dangerous were repeated several times.

Pierre turned back to the ring. What he saw there

made him decide to run for it at once. He grabbed a hat from a man next to him and, keeping his head down, began to elbow his way swiftly to the corner of the tent farthest away from the gendarmes. He would slip quietly under the canvas and then make his way to the border and Belgium as fast as he could.

What he had seen had made him realize he didn't really need to bother about shooting Cyril. It was the same sight that was now keeping 10,000 pairs of eyes excitedly glued to the ring.

When Olaf Lockjaw had seen the dishevelled figure of a chamber-maid climb into the ring he had himself joined in the audience's laughter. No doubt the poor creature was drunk. Or trying to avoid some difficulty with a man. He had walked across the ring with his heavy stride, planning to help the poor woman back through the ropes.

But when he reached her, he found it wasn't a chamber-maid at all. It was a man. Peering close with bloodshot eyes under shaggy brows, he saw it was in fact a sort of clown.

Then Olaf Lockjaw became very angry. So — they wanted to make fun of him, did they? Make fun of the great Olaf Lockjaw, the strongest man in the world? He would show them.

He turned and strode to the side of the ring from which the loudest laughter was coming.

Olaf Lockjaw leaned over the ropes. '*ARRRR-RRRRRHHH!*' he roared, so that several women fainted, and strong men drew nervously back. '*ARRRRRRRRRGHH!*'

Then he turned and with a final and even more terrifying '*ARRRRRRRRRRRRRHHHHHH!*', charged across the ring.

Cyril, who had jumped round nervously at the first roar, saw something much more like a monster than a man coming towards him. Great pounding legs and whirling arms covered in thick black hair, a huge hairy chest bursting out of its leopard skin, and miles above him Olaf Lockjaw's red and bearded face, hardly human in its rage.

Cyril simply shut his eyes and flung himself flat on his face. Olaf Lockjaw charged over him, struck the ropes violently and painfully, and bounced back across the ring.

Now he was more angry than ever. Once more he charged the silly little clown they were all cheering. But by this time Cyril had scrambled up and managed to scuttle out of Olaf Lockjaw's way.

'*ARRRRRRRRRRRHHHH!*' roared Olaf.

Round and round the ring they went — Cyril somehow just managing to avoid the furious giant's enormous grasping hands. The crowd cheered. Olaf bellowed and shook with frustrated rage.

It could not last. Cyril had been absolutely exhausted when he climbed into the ring. Only blind terror kept him going. Turning for the tenth time at a corner, he suddenly felt a finger and thumb grip his shoulder like a giant pair of tongs.

Very slowly Olaf Lockjaw lifted Cyril off the ground and raised him up high above his head.

The great crowd grew deathly quiet. What was

it to be — the broken back, with Cyril smashed down across one of Olaf's huge knees? Or would he simply pull him in half?

It was neither of these. Holding Cyril straight above his head, Olaf Lockjaw began to turn round. Faster and faster he turned, twirling Cyril above him, faster and faster, until he and Cyril seemed a single figure. Faster and faster, spinning and spinning, until they were just a thick, whirling pillar — a blur.

Then, with a flick and a heave, Olaf let go.

Up flew Cyril and out flew Cyril — high over the ropes and the ring and the upturned white faces of the *aaaaaaahing* crowd. Up almost to the roof he went, and then went soaring down the far, far end, the farthest from the door.

Some rents and tears had recently appeared in the canvas roof of this part of the tent and a high, flimsy platform of wooden planks and poles had been erected so that these could be mended.

Fortunately Cyril crashed down heavily on to the top of this and lay, bruised and winded, but not seriously hurt.

The blow, however, was too much for the platform and its slender supporting posts. They all swayed violently from side to side, then three of the spindly poles cracked across, the weight of Cyril and the falling planks cracked four more, and suddenly, with a loud cracking and splitting and splintering the whole rickety structure came collapsing down in pieces to the ground.

Pierre Melon, who was at that moment crawling underneath it to reach the outside, never knew what hit him. One instant he was feeling his way to safety, the next it seemed as if the entire tent had fallen on top of him — knocking him completely unconscious.

There is not a great deal left to tell.

Cyril, once again bruised and shaken and terrified, was actually not too badly hurt. He recovered long before Pierre; in fact, soon after they pulled him from the wreckage.

Some hours later, Deirdre arrived at the gendarme station in Charleville. Kind Chief Inspector Perriot of Nice had brought her up with him in his plane.

After a tearful (on Deirdre's part) reunion between husband and wife, Chief Inspector Perriot sat down to work out what had happened.

It did not take long. Cyril explained his mistake about Pierre Melon and the Beebles, and his other mistake about the sewer exploring club ('Quite natural,' said Chief Inspector Perriot politely, though he was in fact rather surprised). He described how he'd set off the alarm in the bank vault and how he'd left messages all along the road from Nice to Charleville. He was very surprised to learn that as far as Chief Inspector Perriot knew, none of these had been discovered.

Finally, he described the frightful events of the

last few hours. The Chief Inspector was deeply impressed.

'France owes you a debt she can 'ardly repay,' he said. 'Fortunately there ees a reward on the 'ead of the ruffian Melon which will go a leetle way towards eet.'

The next few days were very busy. Cyril and Deirdre spent the night in the grandest room at the Hotel Orange. They learnt there that Gaston and Michel had been caught slipping out of the back by waiting gendarmes. Next morning they flew back to Nice with Chief Inspector Perriot.

Cyril appeared four times on French telly, was interviewed on five radio programmes and in ten newspapers. The newspapers found out all about the other things he'd done — the terrible time he'd been kidnapped and had escaped by blowing up an Arab fort, and the extraordinary adventures he'd had when he'd captured Madam Big.*

The Bank of France gave a dinner for him at which Deirdre was presented with a pearl necklace and Cyril with a jewelled fountain pen, exactly like the ones he'd enjoyed packing in the vault.

And last, there was a huge reception at which Chief Commissioner Durand, Head of the French Gendarmes, handed over a cheque for half a million

* To read about Cyril being kidnapped, see *The Terrible Kidnapping of Cyril Bonhamy* (Evans, 1978). To read about his adventures with Madam Big, see *Cyril Bonhamy v Madam Big* (Cape, 1981; Red Fox, 1990).

francs (about £50,000). Cyril made a short, modest speech in French that was much applauded.

But at last it was all over and Cyril and Deirdre were peacefully alone again in the Hotel Splendide.

'Well, I know what I'm going to do now,' said Cyril when they'd finished breakfast. 'I'm going over to the Bibliothèque de Nice to have a look at those Beebles.'

'Good idea, darling,' said Deirdre. 'But first you must put on one of these,' and fishing about in her handbag she pulled out a brand new little tent of paper, complete with pieces of Elastoplast.

'Why?' said Cyril crossly, looking at the silly thing with disgust. 'What's the point? My nose is fine — look, Deirdre.' And he pointed at his rather large pink nose, which did indeed seem more or less O.K.

But Deirdre was firm. 'Yes — but we don't want you getting sunburnt again, do we?' she said. 'You know what happened last time.'

'Oh, all right, if you insist,' said Cyril. And setting the piece of paper irritably on his nose he set off to see, at long last, the medieval Beebles of Nice.

Other great reads from **Red Fox**

Whatever you like to read, Red Fox has got the story for you. Why not choose another book from our range of Animal Stories, Funny Stories or Fantastic Stories? Reading has never been so much fun!

Red Fox Funny Stories

THANKS FOR THE SARDINE
Laura Beaumont

Poor Aggie is sick and tired of hearing her mates jabbering on about how brilliant their Aunties are. Aggie's aunties are useless. In fact they're not just boring – they don't even try! Could a spell at Aunt Augusta's Academy of Advanced Auntiness be the answer?

Chucklesome stuff!
Young Telegraph

GIZZMO LEWIS: FAIRLY SECRET AGENT
Michael Coleman

Gizzmo Lewis, newly qualified secret agent from the planet Sigma-6, is on a mission. He's been sent to check out the defences of a nasty little planet full of ugly creatures – yep, you guessed it, he's on planet Earth! It's all a shock to Gizzmo's system so he decides to sort things out – alien-style!

0 09 926631 8   £2.99

THE HOUSE THAT SAILED AWAY
Pat Hutchins

It has rained all holiday! But just as everyone is getting really fed up of being stuck indoors, the house starts to shudder and rock, and then just floats off down the street to the sea. Hungry cannibals, bloody-thirsty pirates and a cunning kidnapping are just some of the hair-raisers in store.

0 09 993200 8   £2.99

Other great reads *from* **Red Fox**

Red Fox Fantastic Stories

THE STEALING OF QUEEN VICTORIA
Shirley Isherwood
Boo and his grandmother live above Mr Timms' antique shop. Neither of them has paid too much attention to the old bust of Queen Victoria which sits in the shop – until a strange man offers them some money to steal it for him!
Compelling reading
Book for Keeps

0 09 940152 5   £2.99

THE INFLATABLE SHOP
Willis Hall
The Hollins family is off on holiday– to crummy Cockleton-on-Sea. Some holiday! So one particularly windy, rainy day, it's Henry Hollins' good luck that he steps into Samuel Swain's Inflatable Shop just as a great inflatable adventure is about to begin!
Highly entertaining
Junior Education

0 09 940162 2   £2.99

TRIV IN PURSUIT
Michael Coleman
Something very fishy is happening at St Ethelred's School. One by one all the teachers are vanishing into thin air leaving very odd notes behind. Triv suspects something dodgy is happening. The search is on to solve the mind-boggling mystery of the missing teachers.

0 09 940083 9   £2.99

AGENT Z GOES WILD
Mark Haddon
When Ben sets off on an outward bound trip with Barney and Jenks, he should have realised there'd be crime-busting, top-secret snooping and toothpaste-sabotaging to be done . . .
0 09 940073 1   £2.99

Other great reads from **Red Fox**

Red Fox Animal Stories

FOWL PEST
(Shortlisted for the Smarties Prize)
James Andrew Hall
Amy Pickett wants to be a chicken! Seriously! Understandably her family aren't too keen on the idea. Even Amy's best friend, Clarice, thinks she's unhinged. Then Madam Marvel comes to town and strange feathery things begin to happen.
A Fantastic tale, full of jokes
Child Education
0 09 940182 7   £2.99

OMELETTE: A CHICKEN IN PERIL
Gareth Owen
As the egg breaks, a young chicken pops his head out of the crack to see, with horror, an enormous frying pan. And so Omelette is born into the world! This is just the beginning of a hazardous life for the wide-eyed chicken who must learn to keep his wits about him.
0 09 940013 8   £2.99

ESCAPE TO THE WILD
Colin Dann
Eric made up his mind. He would go to the pet shop, open the cages and let the little troupe of animals escape to the wild.
Readers will find the book unputdownable
Growing Point
0 09 940063 4   £2.99

SEAL SECRET
Aidan Chambers
William is really fed up on holliday in Wales until Gwyn, the boy from the nearby farm, shows him the seal lying in a cave. Gwyn knows exactly what he is going to do with it; William knows he has to stop him . . .
0 09 991150 0   £2.99